To Daisy, Albie and Frank

Mr Tweed and the Band in Need is © Flying Eye Books 2017.

This is a first edition published in 2017 by Flying Eye Books,
an imprint of Nobrow Ltd. 27 Westgate Street, London E8 3RL.

Text and illustrations © Jim Stoten 2017.

Published in the US by Nobrow (US) Inc.
Printed in Poland on FSC® certified paper.

ISBN: 978-1-911171-29-4

Order from www.flyingeyebooks.com

WRITTEN & ILLUSTRATED BY JIM STOTEN

MR TWEED
AND THE BAND IN NEED

FLYING EYE BOOKS
LONDON I NEW YORK

Mr Tweed was at the zoo to hear his favourite jazz band when he came across Wollo the walrus, the band's leader.

"Help, Mr Tweed! I've lost all the band members," said Wollo.

"Cheer up, old chap. We'll find them together! Who should we look for first?" said Mr Tweed.

"The guitar player, Pinky Jackson, should be around here somewhere…" said Wollo.

Can you help them find
the flamingo with a red guitar?

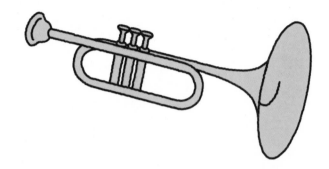

"This is fun! And there's more of us to help search for the others now," said Mr Tweed.

"But we only have until 12 o'clock!" Wollo groaned.

"Don't worry, Wollo!" said Pinky Jackson. "I bet that Jimmy Toots, the trumpet player, is hiding up in the Tall Trees with the other toucans."

There's only one toucan with a yellow trumpet among the trees. See if you can spot him!

Wollo started to feel a lot more cheerful as he followed Mr Tweed, Pinky Jackson and Jimmy Toots further into the zoo.

"We are off to a great start!" said Mr Tweed. "Who's next?"

"I saw Mary Lou Lemur, the saxophone player, somewhere in the Lost Forest," piped up Jimmy.

Listen out for the sweet sounds of
the lemur playing her orange saxophone.
Can you spot Mary Lou?

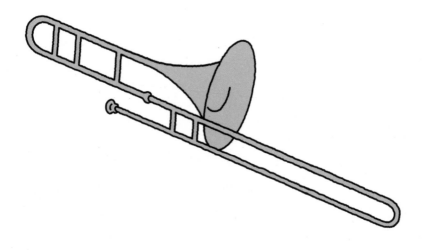

With a growing number of band members beside them, Wollo and Mr Tweed arrived at the Aztec Monkey Trail.

"Ok everyone, keep your eyes open for our trombone player, Otis O'Rangutan! He's sure to be swinging around here," called Mary Lou Lemur.

Can you see an orangutan with a blue trombone among the ancient ruins?

Swinging out of the Aztec Monkey Trail, the party nervously approached the Reptile House.

"Keep your eyes peeled, everyone! Cool Jools, the drummer and the only reptile in the band, should be in here," Otis O'Rangutan murmured.

An iguana with a pink drum kit shouldn't be too hard to find, surely?

The group left the Reptile House and walked through a dark tunnel into the Aquarium. "Who are we looking for?" called Mr Tweed.

"Well…" Cool Jools bellowed. "This is where we should find Jellyfish Jack. He's our banjo player."

Look through the glass with the gang and see if you can spot a jellyfish with a banjo!

They all wandered out of the Aquarium and towards the Arctic Pool. "Only four members left to find! Who's next?" asked Mr Tweed.

"I know!" squeaked Jellyfish Jack excitedly. "This is where Slow-mo Sue, our double bass player, likes to chill out."

It's a bit slippery here, so be careful! But there's a sea lion with a brown double bass somewhere around.

"Oh my!" said Wollo. "It's half an hour to show time!"

"Not to worry, Wollo, old bean!" replied Mr Tweed reassuringly, as they squelched through the mud. "Who's next on the list?"

"I'm sure I saw Hip 'Pop' Thomas, our accordion player, hanging out here in the Mud Pits," said Slow-mo Sue.

Can you find a hippopotamus with a purple accordion?

Slightly muddied, they emerged onto the African Plains.

"Somewhere in this herd is our clarinet player, Zahra Zebra," called out Hip 'Pop' Thomas.

"Ok team, everyone spread out," said Mr Tweed. "We have our work cut out for us here!"

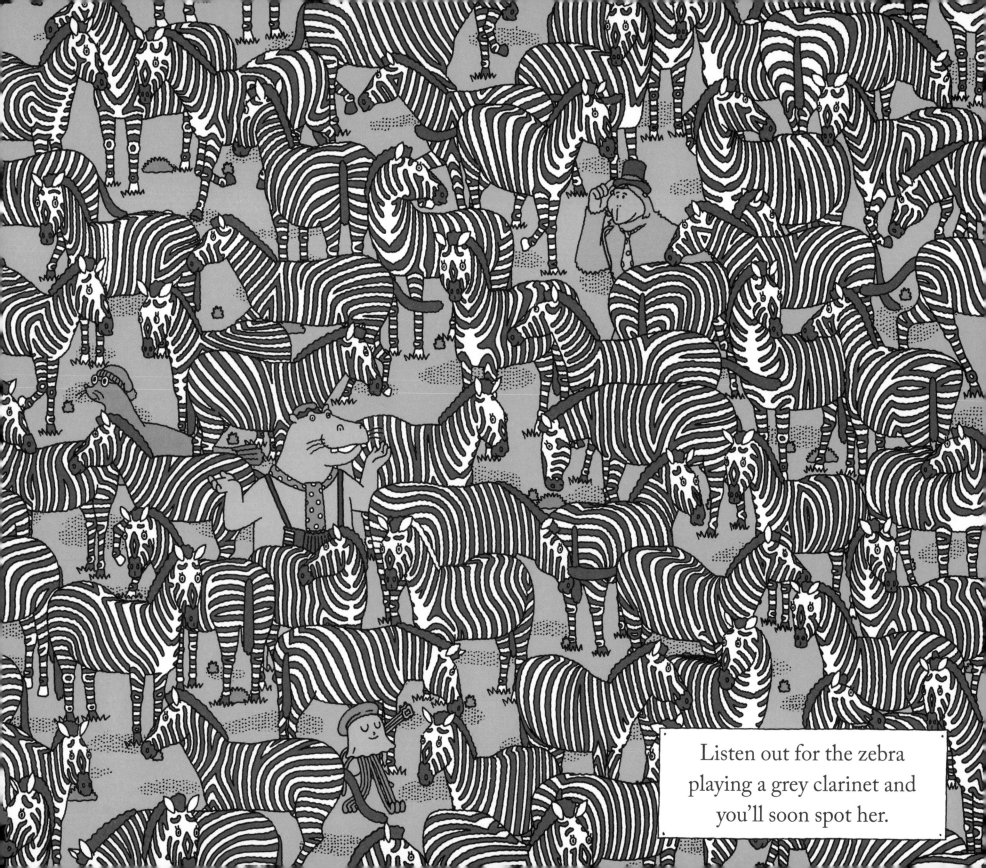

Listen out for the zebra playing a grey clarinet and you'll soon spot her.

Everyone was ready to play, but Wollo still looked worried.

"What's wrong, Wollo? Aren't you excited?" asked Mr Tweed.

"Yes, but… we are still missing the singer, Johnny Cockatoo!"

All of a sudden, a voice joined in with the music…

See if you can find a white cockatoo with a microphone somewhere in the crowd!

"Thank you, Mr Tweed!
See you again soon!"